Tough Jim

By Miriam Cohen

Illustrated by Ronald Himler

Star Bright Books
New York

Published in the United States of America by Star Bright Books, Inc., New York.
The name Star Bright Books and the Star Bright Books logo are registered
trademarks of Star Bright Books, Inc. Please visit www.starbrightbooks.com.

Hardback ISBN-13: 978-1-59572-071-9
Paperback ISBN-13: 978-1-59572-072-6

Previously published under ISBN 002722760X

Printed in China (WKT) 9 8 7 6 5 4 3 2 1

Library of Congress Cataloging-in-Publication Data is available.

For dear Susan, who always knows
where the story is. —M.C.

The first grade was having a meeting
to plan a party. Everyone began talking
about their ideas. George wanted hot
dogs and pizza at the party.

"No!" shouted Danny. "First we have
to say what kind of party it is!"

"It should be a costume
party," said Anna Maria.
"I have a fairy-princess dress.
I'll probably be the prettiest."

But Margaret said, "My dress has a diamond crown. I might be the prettiest." "You can be the smartest," said Anna Maria.

"I'm going to be a hobo," said Sammy.
George said, "I'll be something good to eat."
Danny was smiling. "I'm going to be a
hiccup," he said.

Everyone knew what to be—except Jim.
Paul told them about his monster suit.
"It has hairy fingernails!"
"Quiet!" Danny shouted. "We have
to decide about the party!"

They decided to have cupcakes and
orange juice for each kid in the first grade.
They decided the meeting was over.

"Tomorrow is the party!" everyone
was saying when they went home.

Jim worried about what to be. He wanted to
be someone very strong, someone very tough.

Suddenly he knew!
He rushed to his room
and closed the door.

It was the party day! A big lump of crackly brown
paper walked into the first grade room.
"Ooh, who are you? What are you supposed to be?"
Everyone wanted to know.
"I'm a fried chicken with a crispy crust!
Cluck! Cluck!"

"It's George!" everybody screamed.
"If you are fried, you can't cluck,"
  said Anna Maria.
"You have a good costume, George,"
  said Willy and Sammy.

Anna Maria kept fluffing out her dress. There was real lipstick in her purse. She looked in the little mirror when she needed to put on more lipstick.

Willy and Sammy laughed at each other. Sammy was
a hobo. He had big old shoes with holes in them. He
wriggled his toes out of the holes. Willy had a red rubber
clown nose. When he squeezed it, the nose went "Booop!"

"Hic! Hic! Hic!" Something green
   jumped into the room. It was Danny.
"Danny is hiccuping on us! Make him
   stop!" cried the girls.
   But Danny wouldn't stop.
"Hic! Hic! Hic!"

"Where's Jim?" Paul asked.
"He hasn't come yet," Willy
and Sammy told him.

"When does the eating and drinking begin?"
asked George.
"First we have to arrange everything," said Anna Maria.
She put the cupcakes on the table—first yellows,
then chocolates, then pinks.

A doctor in a white coat kept saying, "Give me your tonsils!"

A creature from space wouldn't talk. Then it said, "It's me! I'm a girl from Mars." It was Sara!

All the first graders were there except Jim.
They were eating and drinking as fast as they could.
Everybody liked their friends' costumes so much.
But they liked their own costumes the best.

Finally, Jim came.
"Hey, Jim, what are you?" Sammy asked.

"I'm a strongman," said Jim. "I saw a picture of 'The Strongest Man in the World' in a book. The helmet wasn't in the picture. I thought of it."

The teacher said, "I like your costume, Jim!
All the costumes are so wonderful."
Then she said, "I have to get a surprise from
my car. Paul, will you help me carry it?"
They left the room.

"Ha! Ha!" said a croaky voice outside the door.
"Strongest man in the world. Ha! Ha!"
A big third grader came into the room.
His name was John Zoogfelder, but his
friends called him Zoogy.

Zoogy walked up to Jim. "You want to fight, kid?"
"Fight?" said Jim. "Why should I want to fight?"
"You're supposed to be tough," said Zoogy.
"Come on, kid."

Zoogy pushed Jim. Then he grabbed Margaret's
crown. Margaret began to cry. Anna Maria
patted her. "Don't cry, honey," she said.
Jim said, "Give Margaret's crown back."
But Zoogy just pulled Jim's helmet over his eyes.

Jim couldn't see. He went crashing around. Anna Maria
lifted her purse to smack Zoogy. Just then, Jim crashed
into Zoogy. Zoogy fell back, right into the wastebasket.
Everyone laughed at Zoogy. He pulled himself out of
the wastebasket and ran out of the room.

"You were too tough for that Zoogy," Margaret said.
And Danny said, "Right into the wastebasket, Mr. Zoogy!"
The teacher and Paul came back with funny hats and a camera.

When everybody told them what had happened,
the teacher put her arm around Jim. She said,
"I don't think Zoogy will bother the first graders
again. Let's not think about it anymore."
Then they got ready to have their party picture taken.

And here it is—
a picture of the whole first grade,
so they could remember their party forever.